This Fairy Tale
Belongs to:

_____

Louis Weber, C.E.O.
Publications International, Ltd.
7373 North Cicero Avenue
Lincolnwood, Illinois 60646

Manufactured in the U.S.A.

8 7 6 5 4 3 2 1

ISBN 0-7853-0484-3

Rumpelstiltskin

Cover illustration by
Sam Thiewes

Book illustrations by
Burgandy Nilles

Story adapted by
Jane Jerrard

Publications International, Ltd.

**L**ong ago, in a time of kings and castles, there lived a poor miller and his beautiful daughter.

The miller was a foolish man who could not stop himself from bragging. His friends told him that his talk would get him into trouble, and they were right.

One day, the miller was lucky enough to meet the King. He bragged to the great man that his lovely daughter could spin straw into gold.

The King, though rich, always wanted more gold, so he asked for the girl to come to his castle that very day.

When the miller's daughter arrived, the King led her to a little room filled with straw. He gave her a spinning wheel and told her that if she could spin all the straw into gold by morning, he would make her his queen. But if she could not, her father must be killed for lying to a king.

He then left the poor girl alone, locked in the little straw-filled room. As soon as he was gone, the miller's daughter sat down and started to cry, for of course she had no idea how to spin straw into gold.

Suddenly the door flew open, and there stood a funny little man, no higher than her waist!

"Good evening, pretty child," he said with a little bow. "What makes you so sad?"

The girl told him about her impossible task, and the terrible fate that awaited her father if she could not spin all the straw into gold.

"Well, I can spin straw into gold," said the little man, as if it were the easiest thing in the world. "But what will you give me for my work?"

"You may have my necklace," said the girl.

And so the little man set to work at the spinning wheel. He spun and spun, and soon the miller's daughter fell asleep. When she woke up at dawn, she was greeted by an amazing sight. During the night, the little man had spun every bit of straw into gold.

The King was amazed to see the spools of gold awaiting him the next morning. But he did not make the miller's daughter his wife. Instead, he took her to a much larger room filled with straw and told her to spin it into gold. If she could not, he warned, her father must be killed.

The poor girl, left alone again, began to cry. She still did not know how to spin gold from straw. Suddenly the door opened and there again stood the strange little man!

"More straw?" he asked. "What can you give me to spin it into gold?"

"The ring from my finger," answered the girl. And so the little man worked all night, and spun every piece of straw into gold.

The next day, the King still could not believe his eyes when he saw the room full of gold. He led the miller's daughter to a third room—one of the largest in his castle—filled to the ceiling with straw. There he left her, and she waited for the little man to appear.

The strange little man came soon enough, but this time the girl had nothing left to give him.

"Give me your first child when you become queen," said the little man.

The girl agreed, for she did not believe she would ever marry the King.

But the next morning, when the King saw the huge room filled with gold, he did marry the girl, and she became the Queen.

A year later, the King and Queen had a beautiful baby. The Queen had forgotten all about her promise to the little man. But the very first day she held her new baby, he appeared once more before her.

"I have come for the child," said the little man.

The Queen wept and begged and offered him all the riches of her kingdom. Feeling sorry for her, the little man told her she could have three days and nights to guess his name. If she guessed right, she could keep her baby.

All that night, the Queen sat up and made a list of every name she knew. Then she sent a servant out to discover new names she had not heard before. The servant roamed the country, asking people their names and making a list for the Queen.

When the little man returned the next evening, the Queen called out names one at a time. "Are you Tom? Dick? Harry?" The little man shook his head.

"Are you Gaspar? Melchior? Balthasar?" But at each name, the little man just smiled and shook his head.

The second day, the servant came back with the strangest names he had heard in the whole kingdom. When the little man appeared that night, the Queen asked him, "Are you Cowribs? Spindleshanks? Lacelegs?"

But he only grinned and shook his head.

The third day, the servant returned with no names at all, but told the Queen a strange story: He had seen an odd little man dancing around a campfire, singing,

"Today I brew, and then I bake,
And soon the Queen's own child I'll take;
For little knows my royal dame
That RUMPELSTILTSKIN is my name!"

That night, the little man came to the palace with a big smile on his face. He was quite certain that the Queen could never guess his name. He asked gleefully if the Queen had any guesses left unguessed.

"Are you Klaus?" she asked.

"No," was his impish reply.

"Could you be Heinz?"

"No," giggled the little man.

"Perhaps you are. . . RUMPELSTILTSKIN?" asked the Queen with a wide smile.

The little man couldn't believe his ears. How could the queen ever have guessed his name? He grew so angry that he stamped his feet until he stamped right through the floor!

And that was the last ever seen of Rumpelstiltskin.